The illustrations in this book were
digitally drawn and painted in Photoshop.

Cataloging-in-Publication Data has been applied for and
may be obtained from the Library of Congress.

ISBN: 978-1-4197-1873-1

Book design by Alyssa Nassner

First published in 2014 by Kinneret, Zmora-Bitan,
Dvir Publishing House Ltd., Or Yehuda, Israel.

Printed and bound in China
10 9 8 7 6 5 4 3 2 1

Abrams Books for Young Readers are available at special discounts when
purchased in quantity for premiums and promotions as well as fundraising
or educational use. Special editions can also be created to specification.
For details, contact specialsales@abramsbooks.com or the address below.

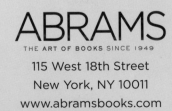

ABRAMS
THE ART OF BOOKS SINCE 1949
115 West 18th Street
New York, NY 10011
www.abramsbooks.com

AN AFTER BEDTIME STORY

by **SHOHAM SMITH**   illustrated by **EINAT TSARFATI**
translated by **ANNETTE APPEL**

Abrams Books for Young Readers
New York

To Sarai, the unsleeping beauty
—From Mom

To Neta, Yair, Yael, Noah, Amit, and Eitan
—From Einat

Our little Nina is fast asleep.

We'll creep away. There's nothing to it . . .

Our little Nina is fast asleep.

"Wait!
Come back!"
she shouts.

How does she do it?

Nina! Stop! It's time for bed!

I don't think she heard a word we said.

Give Aunt Ruth a kiss good night—
then back to bed you go, all right?

No, Nina. No cake! Not one bite . . .

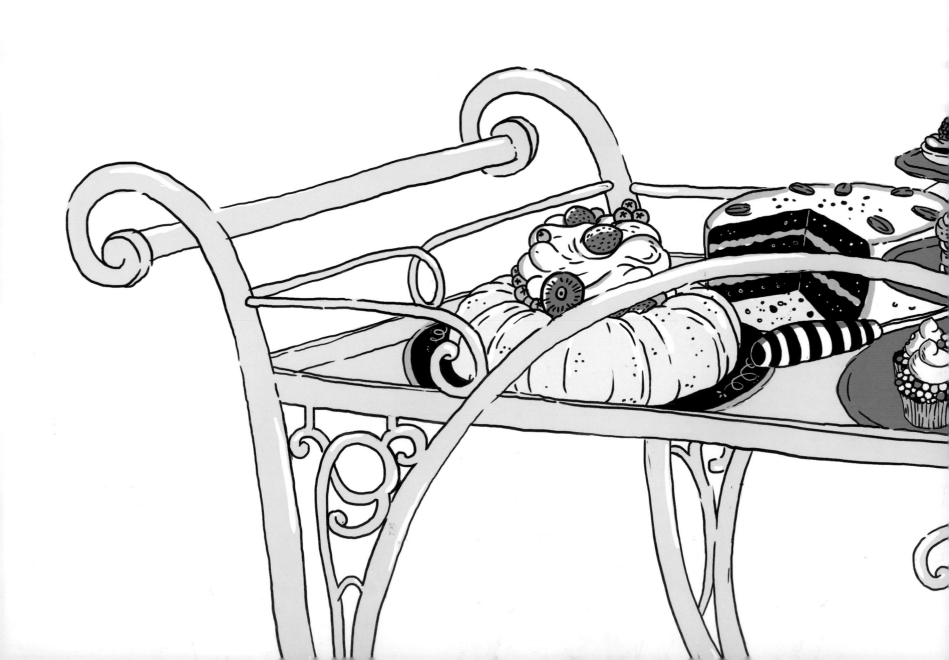

You know we don't eat at this time of night.

Okay . . . Fine . . .
Just one treat.

Careful . . .

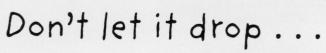

Don't let it drop . . .

Get down, young lady!
That's not how we act.

You're going to bed this instant,
and that's a fact . . .

Come out from under there right away!

That's too much mischief for just one day.

Three!

Uh-oh. We've got company . . .

No!
You cannot gallop down the hall.
Apologize to Uncle Saul!

This is not the time for
saying "Cheese!"

It's time to sleep.
Time to catch some—

Zzzzzzz . . .

So long! Farewell!
A good time was had.

But it's bedtime now
—for Mom and Dad!

Shh . . .